THE HIT-AND-RUN CONNECTION

CAROLE SMITH
Illustrated by Marie DeJohn

ALBERT WHITMAN & COMPANY, CHICAGO

For Ruth Hooker

Library of Congress Cataloging in Publication Data

Smith, Carole.
The hit-and-run connection.

(Pilot books)
Summary: When Ted is injured by a hit-and-run
driver, his friends Jeff and Andy set out
to find the culprit, only to discover he is
a star on their favorite baseball team.
[1. Mystery and detective stories.
2. Hit-and-run drivers — Fiction. 3. Friendship — Fiction] I. DeJohn, Marie, ill.
II. Title.
PZ7.S6436Hi   [Fic]   81-12920
ISBN 0-8075-3317-3 (lib. bdg.)   AACR2

Contents

Chapter 1

THE ACCIDENT

He wished he hadn't stayed so late. The May night was as warm as summer, but Ted Nichols felt an uncomfortable chill as he pedaled his bicycle along the dark road.

Only a few minutes before, he had been having a wonderful time with his two best friends. They had played records as loudly as they pleased because Jeff's parents weren't home to complain. They had turned on all the lights in the house. They had run wildly from room to room, surrounded by dazzling brightness and crashing sound.

Jeff had made popcorn, using lots of butter and salt the way they liked it. Along with that they ate two small cheese pizzas and half a chocolate cake. It was always great to be at Jeff's house because his parents were never home. And his mother left tons of food.

Later, tired and too full to move, they had settled down on the floor to talk. Andy wanted to talk baseball. Ted was tired of talking baseball. Jeff wanted to make up riddles. Andy thought riddles were silly. They argued cheerfully until ten-thirty, time for Ted to leave.

That hadn't seemed very late. Somehow Ted had never expected it would be so quiet once he was away from his friends. Most of the houses on Willow Lane had already turned out all their lights, even though it was Friday night. Darkness made the familiar street seem entirely different. He felt as if he were riding through a time tunnel that would end in some strange place he had never seen before.

A faint clank of metal against metal reminded him that he was only on Willow

Lane, after all. Ted looked to one side, thinking the sound might have been made by a raccoon attacking a garbage can. All he could see was the flatness of a vacant lot broken by a few bushes. They must be lilacs because the sweet smell hung heavily on the still air.

Then a brief spark of light flashed from behind the bushes. Kids camping out overnight, Ted decided. If the other boys had been there, it would have been a good joke to creep around and scare the campers. No fun doing it alone, though.

Too bad he didn't live closer to the other boys. Jeff's and Andy's houses were next door to one another. Ted's house was two miles away. He always felt as if he missed things because he lived so far away. Like the next day—Andy was taking a friend to the baseball game, and the friend was Jeff, not Ted.

Taking a deep breath, Ted pedaled more slowly. Envious thoughts about the game he would see only on television flooded his mind. Jeff and Andy would be there in person.

Behind Ted a car rounded the corner with a screech of tires. He held his front wheel on the white line at the side of the road. He didn't bother to turn off onto the rough shoulder. The lights from the oncoming car caught him, sending his great hunched shadow rushing ahead of him.

The car had plenty of room to pass; no other traffic was in sight. Still, he took a quick glance over his shoulder. A long, pale car was coming up behind him. It was closer than he had expected.

Ted looked again at the road ahead. Too late, he saw the rock that squatted in his path like a fat brown toad. Before he could turn aside, his front tire bounced crazily over it. The handlebars jerked out of his hands.

At first the bicycle shivered, almost balancing on the back wheel. Then it veered left, throwing Ted directly into the path of the car. To his horror Ted felt the jolt of a rushing fender against his body. He went up in the air and slammed down hard, the bicycle on top of him. His right leg crumpled beneath him, and his head rattled against the blacktop.

A brilliant splintering of pain spread through him from head to foot. When it faded away, he felt nothing at all. He couldn't move, but he could hear. He heard the final skid of tires as the car came to a stop. The motor rumbled gently. He heard the car door open and footsteps running to him.

His first thought was to call for help, but he couldn't speak. A rush of sounds poured over him as if someone were talking to him, but Ted couldn't understand the words. Another voice came from the car, or from someplace else very far away.

What was wrong with him? He couldn't move, and he couldn't talk. He couldn't even understand when someone spoke to him. Blackness closed over his head like water rushing over a swimmer, and Ted sank into it.

Saturday morning was bright and sunny. Jeff Lindsey cut across the grass to Andy Ferguson's house, leaving with each step a footprint in the beaded freshness of the dew. Just as he reached the Ferguson driveway, Andy came out.

"I'm all ready," Jeff called. "My parents left to shop as soon as the stores opened, so I thought I'd wait outside. It's better than waiting alone in an empty house."

"Keith will pick us up any minute." Andy ran down the sidewalk toward him. "My mom's on the phone. Something bad must have happened. She kept shaking her head and looking at me funny, so I decided I'd better get out of there."

Jeff stamped his wet feet on the concrete. "I still can't believe your mother knows Keith Owen's mother. And now we're going to a White Sox game with him. I'm sure glad they got him in that trade last winter. He's going to be the best outfielder they ever had."

"I know." Andy's brown eyes snapped with excitement.

"And Julio Viva will be riding with us, too," Jeff continued, awed at the double treat. "I wonder what he'll be like."

Andy frowned. "You should say his name, 'Hoo-lee-o Vee-va.' In Spanish the *j* is pronounced like an *h*. *I* is like *ee*."

"Really?" Then his own name would be

"Heff," Jeff thought. A nonsense riddle began to invent itself in his mind. "What did holly old Heff do with his half a har of ham?"

Before he could decide on an answer with enough J's, a long, light-yellow Cadillac coiled around the corner and into Andy's driveway. With a glad whoop, the boys raced to climb into the back seat.

"Morning." Keith Owen grinned at them over his shoulder. His pale blue eyes and blond hair were a sharp contrast to his darkly tanned face. He looked strong and powerful, and Jeff was impressed. Imagine him, Jeff Lindsey, being that close to a professional baseball player!

"So you're friend Jeff," Keith said with a smile. "Well, meet my friend Julio."

As the small man in the front passenger seat turned, Jeff found himself looking into enormous brown eyes. Tangled strands of black hair fell over a high bulging forehead. The face was more a boy's than a man's, with a narrow jaw and a sharp pointed chin. An odd tension seemed to control the muscles of his face, almost distorting the features. If Jeff hadn't known better, he would have said the ball player was scared to death. Only what could he be afraid of? Julio was a major leaguer. He had it made.

"You're in luck. We're going to have a super game today against Kansas City. Julio's the starting pitcher." Keith headed the car in the direction of the expressway, driving fast. "You should have seen him burn up the league during spring training. He's had two starts since the season began, and two wins. That's pretty good for a rookie. This guy's going to be a sensation. Wait and see. I'm lucky to have him as a teammate and a neighbor."

"I don't think I am so much the pitcher as my friend would say," Julio murmured shyly.

The way he spoke English made Jeff strain to understand, but he didn't mind. He liked the words the way Julio said them.

Settling back into the white leather comfort of his corner of the back seat, Jeff smiled at Andy. Andy smiled back, almost clenching his teeth the way he did when he was really thrilled. It was going to be a fantastic day.

Later, they watched from the bleachers as the team worked out. "I hope Julio's feeling all right," Andy said. He sounded like the anxious father of a little leaguer. "I don't know why he was so quiet today. When I saw him the other night, he did a lot more laughing and fooling around. He'd get excited and forget to speak English. It was funny."

"He's nervous about pitching." Jeff scratched his shaggy brown head, rumpling his hair without noticing. Probably that explained the frightened look he had noticed about Julio.

"I'm glad it's not me," Andy said. "I'd rather be an outfielder like Keith. I'd like to hit home runs the way he does."

In spite of Julio's shyness and nerves, Jeff had felt that the pitcher knew what he was doing. "Well, Julio can handle the pitching. If Keith said he's good, then he must be."

But Julio didn't handle the pitching as well as Jeff and Andy expected. Just before the game began, they took their seats behind the screen. They watched Julio stride out to the mound as if he had been in the big

league for years. The white uniform shirt with its dark blue pants and white socks made him look heavier. His face, shadowed by the bill of his cap, seemed older than it had in the car.

Everyone was surprised when the first batter walked on four straight balls. The second Kansas City batter needed only one pitch to drive the ball into the stands for a home run. As the two opposing players circled the bases in a leisurely trot, Jeff groaned loudly. Andy held his hands over his face so he wouldn't have to watch.

Julio stood beside the mound, staring back toward the bleachers where the ball had fallen. He looked as if he couldn't believe what had happened. The catcher went out to talk to him.

After that Julio got the next three batters on long flies to the outfield. Andy was able to smile again as he marked his scorecard. "We're only two runs down. We can make that up."

Jeff nodded, not worried either. He cheered and clapped with the crowd. Andy tapped his feet in time to the enthusiastic piping from the ball park organ. The next innings passed quickly. Kansas City got several hits and another run. The White Sox had three hits and no runs. Keith had struck out twice, swinging for the fences each time.

In the fifth inning the first Royals batter got a base hit.

"Watch out, Julio," Andy warned, although the pitcher couldn't hear him. "That guy's taking a pretty long lead."

Even before he finished talking, the second batter executed a perfect hit-and-run single. Suddenly runners were on first and third with nobody out.

Julio moved awkwardly, his earlier grace gone. When he pitched again the batter swung hard and the ball sailed toward right field.

"Catch it, Keith," Andy called, jumping up and down. "Catch it!"

The ball slammed into the wall over Keith's head. As it bounced back, he caught it and whirled to throw, but the runner was safe at second. Two runs scored.

"Doesn't look good for Julio." Jeff looked

down to the bullpen,where a relief pitcher was throwing.

Julio allowed another walk. His face was strained. So was the manager's when he came out to talk to Julio. As the manager waved toward the bullpen, Julio started for the dugout with his head bent. He looked small and young again, his confidence gone. Watching him go, Jeff's own stomach knotted in sympathy. Poor Julio.

The relief pitcher struck out the next two batters, making it look easy. The third hitter popped up.

Why couldn't Julio have pitched like that? Disappointed at seeing his new friend outpitched, Jeff sagged in his seat.

"The relief pitcher's Ernesto Seville," Andy told Jeff, writing the name on his scorecard. "He's been around about four years. The manager likes him, but he's never developed the way he should. Julio's been taking his place as a starter."

Suddenly Andy was on his feet, cheering wildly. Jeff jumped up, too. Keith, the Sox lead-off man in the sixth, had smashed a ball into the corner for a triple. He stood smiling at third base, tall and agile, looking exactly the way a ballplayer should look.

The rest of that inning was wonderful and exciting. Batter after batter got on base. Jeff and Andy pounded one another on the back as the fifth run crossed the plate. The Sox had tied the game.

Ernie Seville pitched for two more innings and gave up one run. The Royals were ahead again. Jeff held his breath with every pitch, wondering if he could bear to watch for one more minute.

Only after the Sox got two runs in the eighth inning could he begin to relax. The game ended: Sox 7, Royals 6.

"We won!" Andy jumped up, waving his scorecard.

Jeff stood, too. "It was great! My first major league game." They waited there a few minutes to give Keith and Julio time to shower and change after the game.

Andy glanced toward the television cameramen, who were putting away their equipment. "I hope Ted was watching."

"I meant to jump up and down and wave when I saw the camera on us," Jeff said. "Then I got so interested in the game, I forgot."

Andy had a round face with pink cheeks. Usually he looked cheerful. For just a moment his expression became anxious.

"I'm sorry I couldn't bring Ted, too. I hope he won't be mad. But my mother said Keith was nice enough to offer to take me and one friend, and I shouldn't pester him to take three of us."

Jeff nodded. "Ted will understand. We can at least introduce him to Keith and Julio. He'll probably be waiting for us when we get home."

But when they got home, nobody was waiting for them.

Chapter 2

JEFF DECIDES TO HELP

As soon as Jeff got inside his house, he went to his room. He wanted to put away the autographed ball and White Sox shirt Julio had given him after the game. Considering how disappointed Julio must have been, it was nice of him to have thought of the ball and shirt. Most people wouldn't have. Jeff couldn't wait to show them off to all his friends.

Maybe he could do something to help Julio. Nerves had caught up with him, Jeff decided, remembering a phrase his mother sometimes used. All Julio needed to do was relax and he would start winning again.

Jeff balanced the ball on top of his bookcase and draped the shirt over the bedpost. Then he went back to the kitchen. A peanut-butter sandwich would sure taste good. He had eaten hot dogs all afternoon at the ball park, but the long drive home had made him hungry again.

When the doorbell rang, Jeff took his head from inside the refrigerator. That must be Ted. Somebody would let him in. Too bad he had missed seeing Keith and Julio.

Jeff sprinkled alfalfa sprouts over the peanut butter. On top he laid a piece of buttered bread. His family used sprouts in sandwiches because his mother had heard they were good for you.

They sounded terrible, but Jeff was getting used to them. The only thing he didn't like was the way some of the tiny alfalfas always escaped onto the floor.

The doorbell rang once more, long and impatient. Nobody else had answered. His parents must be away again. It seemed as if they were never home, even on weekends. Sometimes he felt as if he were the only person living in the house. He wished he had a dozen brothers and sisters, so he wouldn't be so lonely.

Jeff grabbed his sandwich and took a big bite on the way to the door. Andy was standing with his nose pressed against the screen.

"Hey, what's up?" Jeff stared at his friend.

He had never seen Andy look so strange. Except for the extra-bright spots of pink on his cheeks, Andy's face was white. He looked like a clown who had put on only part of his make-up.

"Is something wrong?" Jeff set his sandwich on the bookcase. He pushed aside the screen so Andy could come inside.

"It's Ted —" Andy stopped.

"He's mad about not going to the game," Jeff guessed. "That's why he wasn't here waiting for us. Well, you couldn't help it."

He picked up the sandwich. He could eat and sympathize at the same time.

Andy shook his head. There was a shininess in his brown eyes that looked like tears. But Andy never cried.

"That's not it." Andy's voice blared like a broken trumpet. "Ted's in the hospital."

A twist of uneasiness clutched at Jeff's stomach. He dropped the sandwich back onto the bookcase. "What happened?"

"He got hit by a car. On his way home from your house last night."

"Hit by a car? Last night?" Jeff stood still, stunned. "Is — is it bad?"

"Pretty bad." Andy's eyes were blinking very fast. He swallowed again.

That brightness *was* tears. Jeff was amazed, until he felt a dampness in his own eyes. He clenched his fists, trying to think of something else for a minute. All he could think of was Ted's long, solemn face looking the way he had seen it the night before. Ted looked serious even when he was having a wonderful time.

"My mom told me when I got home," Andy said. "She heard this morning, but she didn't want to spoil our day."

"At least he's alive." Jeff took a deep breath. He felt as if he hadn't breathed since he had heard the word *hospital*.

"His parents are with him. He was unconscious for a long time. He has a concussion. And a broken leg. And all sorts of scrapes and bruises."

"Wow!" Jeff was astonished by the weakness in his legs. The stickiness of peanut butter seemed to fill his mouth.

He led Andy into the kitchen and got them both a glass of water. Andy dropped into a chair and drank with long, loud gulps. When he set the glass down, it was empty. Jeff sipped his water more slowly, leaning against the edge of the kitchen table.

"It was hit-and-run," Andy said. "It must have happened soon after Ted left your house. The police said that the driver of another car called them. I guess he saw the bike all mangled in the road, and then he spotted Ted lying in the grass. It's a good thing he called for help!"

"How could anybody hit a kid and just drive on?" Jeff demanded. His shock was turning to anger. "That's a terrible thing to do!"

Andy nodded, tapping his stubby

fingernails against the empty glass. "I know. And it's a crime. Leaving the scene of the accident, I mean. That driver is going to be in bad trouble when they catch up with him."

"Don't they have any idea who it was?" Jeff finally slid into the chair opposite Andy. His legs wouldn't hold him up one second longer.

"There's not a clue." Andy shook his head. "Ted's parents and the police are going to talk to Ted tonight if he's well enough. Maybe he'll be able to give them a lead."

Jeff stared dismally at the floor. "What if he can't? He wouldn't have had a chance to see a license number, or anything like that."

"Well, he must have seen something." Andy sounded more like himself. "He's not some dumb little kid who ran out in the street after a ball. Ted was careful. He had a headlight that worked. And reflectors on his tires."

"There wasn't any moon last night," Jeff said, thinking back. "It must have been pretty dark out there, even if he did have a light." He looked into Andy's wide eyes.

"It must have been scary." Andy's voice was low.

Jeff looked away again, thinking that Ted probably knew the car was going to hit him. How much time would there be to think about it before it happened? He rumpled his thick hair with a trembling hand. He didn't want to let his mind dwell on the car slamming into the bicycle.

"We're going to have to *do* something," Jeff decided. Action was better than thinking. "We're going to have to find out who almost killed Ted."

Andy sat up straight, his mouth suddenly open as wide as his eyes. "How can we find that out?"

"I don't know," Jeff admitted. "But we have to do it. We can't leave Ted in the hospital and not do something to help him. It's bad enough we had the time of our lives today while he was lying there almost dead."

"My mother thought he'd like flowers," Andy said. "She and some of the other mothers are going to order a plant with pretty blossoms. And they're going to make dinners for the family while Ted's mother stays with him in the hospital."

Jeff's mouth curled impatiently. "Flowers and dinners are all right for grown-ups. They're not good enough for us. We have to *do* something."

"It isn't that I don't agree with you." Andy pressed his lips together in a worried line. "But the police are supposed to find out who did it. They go around and ask questions. They put out bulletins. They talk to owners of garages to find out who's having a car fixed."

"But the police don't care as much about Ted as we do... he's *our* friend, and we can investigate, too." Jeff's blue eyes lit with eagerness. "Don't you see? We have to try and help."

"I don't see what we could do that the police couldn't do better." Andy swung his foot back and forth. That meant he was upset. He always swung his foot in school when he hadn't studied the night before and the teacher was asking questions.

Some of Jeff's enthusiasm faded, but he

wouldn't give up. "We should at least try. Let's go see where it happened. Maybe we'll get some ideas if we see the place."

"I don't know where it was," Andy told him. "All I know is that Ted was about halfway home."

Jeff stood up. "Let's get our bikes and ride the way Ted would have gone last night. There must be something that will show the spot."

Andy stood, too, although he didn't act convinced. "Okay. We can ride over that way, I guess. But I can't stay long, I have homework."

They rode to Willow Lane and turned in the direction of Ted's house. The lane was narrow and had no sidewalks. The houses were set far back from the road on large lots. Big old trees and tall bushes grew along the roadside. Even in the late afternoon sunshine, Willow Lane seemed remote and lonely.

Chapter 3

THE SEARCH FOR ROOM 311

Halfway to Ted's house Jeff and Andy began to ride as slowly as they could. Their eyes scanned the blacktop, searching for some sign of the accident. Everything looked so ordinary that Jeff began to think they had missed the place.

Up ahead was a driveway where two little girls were playing with doll furniture. When the boys reached them, Jeff stopped to talk. Andy waited just ahead, acting as if he didn't want to be seen talking to little girls.

"Hey," Jeff said to the children, "do you know where the kid was run over last night?"

One little girl looked at him for a long

moment. Without making any answer, she lowered her blond head to her doll bed. Tenderly, she lifted out a caramel-colored toy bear and held it against her chest. The bear was wearing red and white striped pajamas.

Jeff blinked once with surprise before he turned to the second girl. She was patting the quilt on her bed around a lump of something fuzzy.

"Did *you* hear about the accident?" he asked. "Where did it happen?"

The little girl turned her head so fast her long brown hair flopped on her shoulders. "Down there." She pointed down Willow Lane in the direction of Ted's house.

At least they hadn't passed it, Jeff thought, glad to know that much. "Which side?" he persisted.

This time she didn't answer. Just when he had given up expecting any more help, she said, "This side. Past the vacant lot."

"Thanks." Jeff smiled at her.

She didn't smile back. She was busily arranging the quilt on her doll bed. A cloth fur head with one bright eye showed on the pillow, and pointing out below the eye was a long orange beak. In surprise, Jeff realized that her toy was a stuffed penguin.

They rode on until just beyond the vacant lot Andy called, "Look!" He got off his bike, laid it down on the grass, and stooped over, staring down at the road.

There was no doubt about it. Andy had found skid marks. Jeff looked for cars. None were coming from either direction, so he got down on one knee. Extending a finger, he ran it gently over the rough blacktop. Sparkling fragments of glass clung to the finger.

"This is where it happened all right," Jeff said. "That little girl knew what she was talking about."

"They've cleaned it up." Andy bent down beside him. "Except they didn't quite get all these little bits of glass. I wonder where it all came from?"

"It must be from Ted's light. Or from one of the car headlights."

"The police probably have the bigger pieces," Andy decided. "And the bicycle,

what's left of it. There's nothing we can do."
He stood up and headed for his bike.

Jeff watched him, beginning to feel
helpless. The smell of freshly cut grass
from the front lawn of a small white house
mingled with the sweet smell of lilac bushes
along the road. Everything was perfectly at
peace, and he couldn't help but think
Andy was right. There was nothing they
could do.

But all day Sunday, instead of making up
riddles as he usually did in his spare time, Jeff
thought about Ted—lying in the hospital. He
wasn't going to give up. There had to be some
way they could help Ted.

Before the day was over, he had an idea.
That was why on Monday after school he and
Andy walked through the front entrance of
the city hospital.

"Well, here we are. But we don't have to
stay." Andy glanced hopefully at Jeff. "We
could go across the street and get our ice
cream instead."

"We'll do that later," Jeff said. "I promised
I'd buy you a shake if you'd come with me,

and I will. But not until we've seen Ted."

He took three steps forward and stopped, wrinkling his nose. "What's that smell?"

"Disinfectant," Andy told him. "All hospitals smell of it. Haven't you ever been in a hospital before?"

"No," Jeff admitted, "I never have."

"Well, that's it then." Andy suddenly seemed more relaxed.

"That's what?" Jeff asked.

"That's why you were so anxious to come here. You don't know anything about how hospitals are run. You don't know how fussy they are. I know because I was in one when I was four. They took out my appendix."

Looking around, Jeff had to admit he was curious. But that wasn't why he had insisted on coming. He had wanted to come because he still thought they should look for the car that had hit Ted.

As soon as they heard Ted's story, they would have the same clues to work with that the police did. With those clues they could start to search — on their own.

At the moment they were standing on the

edge of a cheerful waiting room. It had comfortable blue chairs and lemon yellow couches. In one corner a frail man in a bathrobe and slippers sat in a wheelchair talking to a man wearing sunglasses and holding a briefcase.

Nobody else was in sight except a black-haired woman in a bright pink coat who was seated at a desk located at the far end of the room.

The woman's hands were clasped on the cleared surface in front of her. On her face was the expression of a school principal about to tell a boy he was in serious trouble.

"We're never going to get past her." Andy shook his head and half-turned to leave. "You have to be sixteen to be a visitor here."

"Wait!" Jeff grabbed Andy's arm. "We know Ted is in Room 311. There must be some way to get to that room without attracting attention."

"You see that lady? Well, she has to give every visitor a card. And she won't give us one because we're too young. Hospitals don't like kids unless they're sick."

Jeff had to agree that their idea seemed hopeless. The woman's desk was directly across from the elevators. If they walked over and tried to get on one, she would stop them. She would ask their ages and they would have to say twelve, not sixteen.

Once she knew how young they were, she would refuse to give them a pass and they would have to go. So they would be at another dead end, just as they had been at the scene of the accident.

They would have to wait to talk to Ted, and then it would be too late to help. The hit-and-run driver would have had time to hide all the evidence against him. Or the police would have solved the case.

Suddenly Jeff's eyes brightened. He made one more quick examination of the woman and her desk and the elevators. Beyond that area the corridor ended at a wide closed door. A large sign over it said "X ray."

Maybe there was a way to get to Ted after all.

"Walk straight ahead with me as if you knew where you were going," he told Andy.

Andy hesitated, making no move to do as Jeff had told him. Jeff started out, anyway. He kept his eyes on the sign he had noticed beyond the elevators. Good old Andy caught up with him.

They moved purposefully, but not too fast. From the corner of his eye Jeff could see the woman's head turn to watch them.

As they passed the desk and the elevators and reached the closed door, her sharp eyes stabbed at them. Jeff felt as if she must be reading his mind, but he kept going. As casually as if he had done it a hundred times, he pushed the swinging door and sauntered through. Andy followed him, cheeks flaming. Behind them the door swung slowly shut.

With a great sigh of relief Jeff sagged against the wall. They were alone in a long corridor. Ahead of them a green arrow pointed to the X-ray Department.

"What did we just do?" Andy demanded with a nervous laugh. "Where are we? Why didn't she stop us?"

Jeff grinned. "I got the idea when I saw the sign. People come from all over to have X rays taken. They don't have to be patients in the hospital. And they aren't visitors. I thought it was worth a chance, and it worked. She didn't ask us any questions because she thought we were going to X ray."

"But we don't want an X ray."

"No," Jeff agreed, "but we do want a stairway. Or another elevator. We have to get up to the third floor somehow."

"What if there isn't a stairway or an elevator?" Andy's dark eyes bulged. "What if a doctor or a nurse comes along and asks where we think we're going?"

"Look as if you need an X ray. Limp. I'm sure if we just walk slowly down this hall, nobody will think a thing about us."

Andy began to drag his left foot. They moved slowly, passing a number of doors with complicated names on them. The green arrow turned a corner at the end of the long hall, so they did, too.

"I thought of a riddle," Jeff announced.

Andy's head jerked with surprise.

"What did the man in the wheelchair say to his girl friend?"

"This is not the time for riddles," Andy hissed. He looked longingly back the way they had come.

"He said, 'I'm a PUSHover for you, dear,'" Jeff announced with a broad grin. "Isn't that pretty good?"

"Not really." Andy clenched his teeth and stopped in front of a single elevator with an extra-wide door.

"Must be for patients on stretchers,"Andy said. "We wouldn't dare use it."

Jeff went to the panel and pushed the button. At once the door slid silently open.

"Get in." Jeff pushed at Andy.

Andy wouldn't be pushed. "I don't want to."

Jeff stepped inside alone. "I'm going up to see Ted. You can go back to the waiting room if you want. I'll see you later."

Looking over the row of buttons, he found the one marked *Three*. No matter how confident he had tried to sound, he felt shaky. If Andy didn't come with him, he didn't know if he would have the nerve to press the button and go upstairs all by himself.

Chapter 4

TED'S CLUE

Taking a deep breath, Jeff made his finger push the button marked *Three*. Just before the elevator door closed, Andy jumped inside with him.

"This is crazy," Andy said. "I don't know why I'm keeping you company like this. We're going to get in terrible trouble, I just know it."

But Andy couldn't help smiling. He and Jeff stood there, grinning at one another, until the elevator stopped and the door opened again.

A young girl in a pink-and-white striped uniform was waiting to get on. They stepped out, their faces suddenly very serious.

The girl looked at them curiously, her lips

parted as if she intended to ask a question they couldn't answer. But when the elevator door started to close, she rushed to get inside. Whatever she had meant to say was forgotten.

"That was a close call." Jeff closed his eyes for a moment, taking a deep breath.

Then he looked down the long corridor that stretched ahead of them. Instead of the stillness along the X-ray hall, the sound of voices came from several directions.

"Where are we now?" Andy sounded unhappy again.

Jeff shrugged. He rumpled his hair with one hand as he thought what to do next.

"I think we should walk down to the end of this hall and see what's there. Didn't you say Ted was in the children's ward?"

The boys started walking down the hall.

"That was Room 351," Andy whispered, looking at a nearby door.

They went through a swinging door and stopped to listen. A baby was crying in the distance. A child's voice came from the room nearest to them.

"This is the children's ward!" Jeff felt as elated as if he had made it to the moon. "And we're outside Room 316. Hurry, Andy. We're awfully close. We don't want to be stopped now."

They weren't stopped. They slipped as silently as young ghosts into Room 311. Two beds were lined along one wall. Two chairs and two metal tables stood between them.

In the bed nearest the door lay a child with long, tumbled rust-colored hair. Jeff wasn't sure whether the person was a boy or girl, but he did know it wasn't Ted.

Beside the window was a long figure with its head wrapped in bandages. That didn't look like anyone Jeff knew, either. He had to look twice before he recognized the big nose and the wide cheekbones.

Jeff nudged Andy, who jumped. "That's him."

They tiptoed across the floor. The boy with the tangled hair rolled over on his back. His eyes looked directly at them, but he seemed strange and sleepy. He didn't seem to see them at all. Jeff hoped that Ted was going to be more wide awake than that boy.

"Ted." He spoke in a low voice, stopping beside the second bed.

The eyes that opened were big and brown and sad, the way Ted's always looked. They were confused, too, as if they didn't believe what they saw. Jeff realized he had never seen Ted without his glasses before. Come to think of it, he had never seen Ted sick.

"It's us, Ted," Jeff said, forgetting to whisper. "Andy and Jeff. We wanted to see how you were."

"Hi." Ted's voice was a faint croak. He

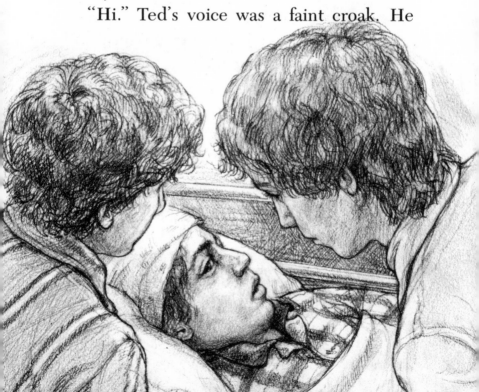

tried to smile and failed. "How'd you guys get here?"

"It wasn't easy," Jeff told him. He fumbled in his jacket pocket and thrust a paper bag at Ted. "Here. I thought you could use this."

Ted felt for the bag with one hand, but he didn't try to open it. He seemed mixed up.

"It's my transistor radio," Jeff explained. "With the earplug. I thought you might like to borrow it while you're here. You can listen to some good music."

Ted finally seemed more alert. He patted the paper bag with his left hand. His arm looked thinner than Jeff remembered. The broad band of the wristwatch Ted was still wearing seemed too heavy for the slender arm.

"Thanks, Jeff. I haven't heard a tune with a beat since—"

He stopped. Jeff knew he was remembering the night of the accident.

"Andy and I want to help you," Jeff said quickly. "Can you answer some questions?"

Ted's eyes closed slowly and then fluttered open. "I don't remember much about what happened. I was just riding along, minding my own business, and pow! That's all I know." His voice faded.

"What else, Ted?" Jeff leaned forward eagerly. "Don't you remember anything else? What kind of car was it that hit you?"

"I don't know." Ted looked sadder than ever. "My head still hurts. I have trouble thinking about the accident."

"Sure. That's okay, Ted." Jeff made an effort to hide his disappointment.

When Ted didn't say anything more, Andy stepped forward. He looked uncomfortable.

"I'm sorry you didn't get to the baseball game with us, Ted. I brought you a ball. Autographed by the whole team. And when you're well enough, Keith promised he'd take all three of us to a game."

"Thanks, Andy. I'd like that." Ted didn't seem especially interested, though. He closed his eyes again.

"Well, we'll see you later," Jeff said, feeling that they should leave.

"Good-by." Ted didn't urge them to stay. He didn't even open his eyes.

His mouth turned down in defeat, Jeff hesitated. At last he shrugged and gave up. Poor Ted. It was too bad, but they weren't going to be able to help him.

"Jeff?" Ted's faint call stopped him.

"I do remember one thing," Ted whispered. "About the car. I saw it just before it hit me. It was long. Maybe a Lincoln. Or a Cadillac. And it was a light color, I think."

Ted licked his lips and shuddered. He squeezed his eyes even more tightly shut.

Jeff and Andy went quietly away. Andy looked as if he were going to be sick, but Jeff was smiling. They had the clue they needed! They had a description of the hit-and-run car.

For the next two days the boys rode their bicycles around their small suburban town, looking for light-colored cars.

They concentrated on spotting white, beige, and yellow Cadillacs and Lincolns. There didn't seem to be many of them in the area. And they didn't see even one in any of the repair shops they visited.

On Thursday they met in Jeff's front yard

after school. Jeff was as enthusiastic about the search as he had been since the beginning. To his amazement Andy didn't appear especially eager to get going.

While Jeff waited impatiently, Andy scuffed across the thick grass. "My mother talked to Ted's mother today," he announced.

"What'd she have to say? Did she find out we visited him?"

"Ted's feeling better. And I don't think his mother knows we were there."

Jeff closed his eyes and made a soundless "Whew!"

"The police are still investigating," Andy continued. "They have some paint chips from the hit-and-run car. Ted's mother didn't say what color they are. And the police have what's left of Ted's bike. It was *his* light that broke. They are working hard to find the car."

"That's interesting." Jeff reached into his pocket for a package of gum he had bought after school. He offered a piece to Andy.

"Do you have the feeling it means something? I mean, that nothing's been found. Maybe the car's from another suburb or a different state. Maybe nobody will ever see it again, not even the police. Or maybe it's hidden somewhere."

"I'll bet it is hidden." Andy took the gum, looking more interested. "The police are sure the right front fender is badly damaged. If I'd done it, I wouldn't let anybody see that car for years."

"Well, then that's what we have to do today," Jeff decided. "Look for a hidden car. We'll check all the out-of-the-way places we can think of." He unwrapped a stick of gum for himself and stuffed it into his mouth. The sharpness of cinnamon pricked his tongue as he began to chew.

"Okay. That sounds pretty good." Andy chomped with exaggerated fierceness. His eyes slid away from Jeff's.

"But I don't want to spend any more time looking for the car after today. The police are working on the case. They can find out more than we can. I'd rather work on my social studies project. I'm going to make a really good exhibit for our unit on South America."

"You can do that project in half an hour,"

Jeff protested. He knew because that was how long he had spent. In fact, he had done it the night before while his parents went to a movie.

"I know. But I don't want to." Andy's cheeks grew pink. "I'd like to help Ted. And I know you would, too. But there isn't anything we can do. So I'd rather spend the time on my project. And I want to learn more baseball rules and batting averages. I'm going to the game again Friday night."

As determined as he was to find the hit-and-run car, Jeff was distracted by the mention of the baseball game. But Andy didn't say anything about inviting him.

"Why don't you think we can help Ted?" he asked.

"Because we'd be borrowing trouble," Andy burst out. "I think we should mind our own business."

Jeff thought that over. Finally, he said, "Well, let's not waste any more time today. Let's get moving."

Andy was a good guy. Jeff knew he would come around.

Chapter 5

BABY-SITTERS

For two hours Jeff and Andy rode around town to the loneliest places they could find.

During their explorations they discovered three abandoned stoves and one refrigerator without doors. In a culvert lay a discarded mattress and springs. Behind a concealing clump of bushes was a rusting car of uncertain age and color that must have been there for years. But nowhere did they see any sign of the car they were looking for.

Even Jeff felt discouraged when they pedaled back along their street. Because Andy's mother was standing on the Fergusons' front porch, looking serious, Jeff didn't stay to talk. He went straight home.

Since his parents were still at work, he decided to mow the lawn while he waited for them to get home. While he mowed, he could think about where to look for that car next. He wished he could talk Andy into helping a little longer.

Dragging the lawn mower, he backed out of the garage. Andy came racing across the lawn toward him.

"Jeff! Jeff!" he bellowed. "How would you like to baby-sit tonight?"

"Baby-sit?" Jeff's lip curled. "Are you kidding? Me? Baby-sit?"

Andy laughed and explained. "Keith called. He said Julio is pretty unhappy. He started the game this afternoon and allowed four runs in the first inning. Didn't even get three outs before they yanked him."

"Oh, no. That's bad." A strange rush of feeling swept Jeff. It must be scary to be so near great success, and then to fail. He suddenly remembered that he had intended to find some way to help Julio. In the excitement about Ted he had forgotten all about the pitcher.

"Keith wants to take Julio and his wife out to dinner to cheer him up," Andy continued. "But they can't unless somebody will stay with their little boy. Keith thought we might take the job."

Jeff hesitated. Since he had no brothers or sisters, he wasn't used to small children. Still, he wanted to help Julio any way he could. "I don't know. How old is the kid?"

"About three or four, I think."

"Well, that sounds okay, I guess." Jeff headed the lawnmower back into the garage. "If we don't have to change any diapers. And if it's all right with my mother."

The more he thought about it, the more interesting the job sounded. He had never seen a major league ballplayer's house before. He knew that Julio lived near Keith, but he didn't know just where.

Jeff ran inside, telephoned his mother, and received permission to go. Then he called Andy back. Keith would pick them up at six-thirty. That meant Jeff would have to make his own supper. He grilled cheese sandwiches, using plenty of cheese.

His mother came home just in time to make him a fruit salad. She put in mostly banana, which he didn't like. Because there was no time to argue, Jeff had to eat it. "Almost like blackmail!" he thought.

At six-twenty-five he was ready and outside, waiting with Andy for Keith to arrive.

Six minutes later the long, pale yellow Cadillac pulled up at the curb. Andy opened the door to the backseat and scrambled in.

About to follow, Jeff stopped suddenly. The car they had been searching for was a long, light-colored Cadillac or Lincoln. And here was a Cadillac they had never even thought of. Even though it was Keith's car, they should check it for dents on the right front fender.

"Come on," Andy said. "What are you waiting for?"

Jeff knew he couldn't go around the open door to look at the fender without saying what he was doing. And he could hardly tell Keith his car was a suspect.

"Hi, there," Keith said in his friendly way. "How are you doing?"

He looked great in a yellow sports jacket that somehow seemed just right with his jeans. They were expensive faded ones that exactly matched his eyes. Jeff wished he had a pair of jeans like Keith's — he had blue eyes, too, didn't he? He shrugged and got in. He would have to look at the fender later.

"Thanks for doing us this favor," Keith told them. "Julio and his wife can really use a little time to relax. He's scared to death of being sent back to the minors right after he thought he was making it in the big league."

"I sure hope nothing like that happens," Jeff said. "But I know he'll settle down soon."

"One day he was taking the whole big league bit in stride and the next he was a nervous wreck." Keith jerked his head with irritation.

He roared off down the street and turned onto Willow Lane without braking. "The shock of really being with the Sox seemed to hit Julio all at once, and he can't shake it."

Jeff didn't pay much attention to what Keith was saying. He couldn't keep his mind off Keith's car being long and light-colored.

And they were whizzing down lonely Willow Lane toward the very spot where Ted had been hit. With a sigh, Jeff adjusted his seat belt and silently wished that Keith wouldn't drive so fast.

"Did you have a home game last Friday night?" he asked suddenly.

"No," Keith answered right away. "We were in Detroit."

"That's good," Jeff muttered. He gave a sigh of relief. No need to check the Cadillac after all. Keith couldn't have hit Ted. Not if he had been out of town.

"Well," Keith went on, "we would have been in Detroit if there'd been a game. Actually, it poured all day and the game was called. We caught an evening flight back to Chicago. I was home early. Too late to call Barbara, though, so I went... Well, you wouldn't be interested in that."

Dismayed that Keith couldn't be crossed off after all, Jeff sank back in the comfortable seat. Andy was looking at him closely, a frown wrinkling his high forehead. He must have figured out what Jeff was getting at.

"Hey, speaking of games," Keith said, "would you guys like to go to the game with the Cleveland Indians tomorrow night? I heard you don't have school in the afternoon. You could drive in with me and Julio again. Since Julio and I live near each other, we like to share rides to the ball park."

"Great!" Andy exploded. About to say more, he stopped to glance uneasily at Jeff.

"I wouldn't mind going," Jeff said slowly.

"Well, that's fine. Pick you up about two." Keith didn't seem to notice Jeff's hesitation.

Just before they came to the place where Ted had been hurt, Keith spun the car into a fast right turn. He drove a short block and turned left. After half a block he braked sharply and shot into a cement driveway. Julio's house was a small, brown ranch in a big yard with velvety green grass and tall old trees.

As soon as they got out, Julio opened his front door. A small boy ran on short, skinny legs to meet them. Keith lifted him up in his arms and swung him around while the little boy gurgled with laughter.

Keith set the child back on his feet. "This is Paco. Paco, meet Andy and Jeff."

A pair of curious dark eyes looked up at them from beneath a fringe of black hair. Paco smiled, showing perfect tiny teeth.

Soon Julio came down the drive with a slender young woman almost as tall as he was. She looked calm and at ease compared to Julio, who seemed as tight as a stretched guitar string.

Julio sure was taking losing hard, Jeff thought, but he understood how important winning had to be. Getting attention, making people proud of you — those things meant a lot to him, too.

Julio put one arm around Keith. "This man is some kind of good friend, you know? I would do anything for this man."

Looking a little embarrassed, Keith introduced Teresa, who told them about Paco. The boys didn't have to do much to take care of him. The only part Jeff didn't like was having to read bedtime stories. But Paco was only three, and Teresa said it was the best way for him to practice English.

As Keith and Julio and Teresa got into the car, Andy picked up Paco so he could wave good-by. That was when Jeff finally had a chance to wander casually toward the right front fender of Keith's car. He felt like a rotten friend, but he did it.

What if the fender were dented? What would he do? Could he actually call the police and tell them to see if their paint chips matched Keith Owen's car?

The Cadillac pulled away just as Jeff came to a stop beside the gleaming fender. He stood still, watching it go.

"Well?" Andy demanded. "What did you see? Was it dented?" He sounded mad.

"No," Jeff said, surprised. "It was okay."

Andy's cheeks were flaming. "You should have known it would be. What's wrong with you? After Keith was nice enough to take you to a baseball game. After he liked you and invited you to go again. How can you suspect him of running over Ted?"

He set Paco on his feet with a bump.

"I didn't think Keith did it," Jeff protested, getting angry, too. "But he drives the kind of car we're looking for. I had to make sure, didn't I? Don't you think I'm really glad his fender was smooth and shiny?"

Andy didn't get a chance to answer. Paco stood with his tiny track shoes set wide apart, looking from one to the other. Without warning he began to scream.

"What's wrong with him?" Jeff took a quick step backward.

"I don't know." Andy forgot about being mad at Jeff. He got down on his knees and tried to put his arms around Paco. Paco shrugged away, screaming even more loudly.

"You try it," Andy said to Jeff. He shoved Paco in Jeff's direction.

Jeff patted the small boy clumsily on the back. "Hey, Paco, it's okay."

"You're treating him like a puppy," Andy criticized.

"I don't know what else to do with him," Jeff explained. He kept on patting, and Paco stood still. He stopped screaming, but big tears poured down his chubby cheeks.

Just before Jeff and Andy could begin a new argument about what to do next, a little girl came from behind the house and walked up to them.

"What did you do to Paco?" The small child sounded like a mother who thought her child was being mistreated.

"We didn't do anything," Jeff protested.

Where had he seen that girl before? Something about her seemed familiar. His eyes dropped to the large stuffed toy bird she held in her arms.

"Paco," she said sweetly, turning to the younger child, "you can hold Penguin if you stop crying."

Paco sniffed and opened his eyes. Then he held out his arms for the toy. Good as her word, the little girl thrust the bird at him.

"Mr. Propper is working on his telescope," she said next. "Let's go over and help him. Penguin likes to help Mr. Propper."

Without a glance at the big boys, the two children tramped across the grass toward the house next door. Jeff and Andy trailed along behind, careful to keep a safe distance away. If the little girl had soothed Paco, they didn't want to do anything to set him off again.

Chapter 6

MR. PROPPER'S TELESCOPE

There had been so much confusion, with the grown-ups leaving, and with Paco's tantrum, that neither Jeff nor Andy had noticed the man working next door. He was setting up a telescope in his driveway.

"Hi, Mr. Propper," called the little girl.

"Hello, Allison," answered the tall, gray-haired man. "Hello, Paco. Who are your friends?" He looked over their heads at the big boys.

Jeff smiled and came nearer. He always enjoyed meeting someone new. "We're Andy Ferguson and Jeff Lindsey. We're taking care of Paco."

"Glad to meet you." Mr. Propper smiled back. He had a small gray mustache that stretched when he moved his lips. "Don't worry about Paco. He's usually a very well-behaved boy. And he's smart. He just gets confused sometimes when you speak English too fast. He doesn't always understand."

"So that's why he was crying." Jeff felt better. "We were talking pretty fast. I guess he couldn't keep up with what we were saying."

"He's fine now," Mr. Propper assured them. "Just remember to speak simply and slowly and he won't have any trouble understanding." His attention returned to Paco and Allison and he asked with a grin, "Who wants to be the first to look through the telescope?"

"Me!" shouted Allison.

Paco grinned and began to jump up and down. Handing the big stuffed penguin back to Allison, he raised his arms to be picked up.

Mr. Propper lifted him so he could see through the shining tube that was aimed across the street. They couldn't tell what he was seeing, but he giggled as if he liked it.

"My turn." Allison forgot to be motherly and butted her bird against Mr. Propper's leg.

She took a long look. Then she insisted that Penguin look, too. That was when Jeff remembered where he had seen her before.

It had been last Saturday when they were trying to find the spot where Ted had been run down. Allison and her friend had been playing on Willow Lane about a block away.

That meant Ted had been hit not far from Julio's house. He wondered how far.

He was trying to figure it out when Mr. Propper set Allison and Penguin on the ground. The little boy and girl ran off to roll and tumble on Mr. Propper's beautiful sloping lawn. Carefully placed against a tree trunk so he could watch was the penguin. Jeff didn't know how he could have forgotten that stuffed bird with its wickedly shining eyes.

"What do you use that telescope for?" Andy asked Mr. Propper.

"Astronomy. I retired a few months ago," Mr. Propper explained, resting a hand on the gleaming black and silver apparatus. "My wife bought me this telescope for my birthday. Now I've become an amateur astronomer.

"I never knew retirement was going to be so much fun. Since Julio rented the house next door, I've become a baseball fan, too. There's a lot of strategy to baseball that I never appreciated before."

"There sure is," Jeff agreed. "I used to

think that one guy threw the ball while another tried to hit it and the others just stood around waiting to catch it. But every play is really different, and there are all sorts of reasons for what the players do."

"I like astronomy, too," Andy interrupted. "I've read a lot about outer space. And I like looking at all those little sparks of light and knowing the stories about them."

"Those stories were an amusement for people centuries ago," said Mr. Propper. "They thought they saw people and animals in the patterns of the stars. So they named them and made up tales about them."

"The first star to look for in the night sky is the North Star," Andy said, showing off a little. "It's the brightest and easiest to find. It stays in the same place all night long and through the seasons, while the other stars seem to circle around it. That's how travelers long ago found their way over lands and seas they had never seen before."

"Isn't it strange," commented Mr. Propper, "how you can walk under the night sky for years and never pay attention to it? I had only a vague idea about the map that's up there, and I'd forgotten the few stories I'd heard. That's why it seems exciting to me now."

Jeff felt uncomfortable. He was one of those people who never noticed things like stars. Maybe he was missing something.

"I've been studying for weeks." Mr. Propper looked at Jeff as if he understood exactly how he felt. "I've only been going out to look at the sky the past few days. There's a vacant lot on Willow Lane just behind our house, and that's where I often set up my telescope. Nights when there is no moon are the best. I've seen a lot already."

They stayed talking to Mr. Propper until Andy noticed it was time to take Paco inside to get him ready for bed.

As soon as they called his name, the little boy ran to them. He seemed to understand what they said about bedtime, but suddenly he darted away.

"Paco," Jeff called. He wondered if he should chase the little fellow and carry him home. Maybe Paco was one of those children who hated to go to bed. Jeff wasn't sure if he could listen to more wailing and watch more tears. Maybe they should let him stay up longer. No, that wouldn't be right. They shouldn't let him break his mother's rules.

"He has to get his Big Wheel," Allison explained just before Jeff took off after Paco. She picked up Penguin and gave the bird a tender pat on its head.

"His what?" Jeff stopped to stare at her.

"His Big Wheel." Allison repeated the words patiently. "He's supposed to put his toys away before he goes inside."

Understanding at last, Jeff and Andy said good night to Mr. Propper and went to help Paco. He had dragged the wide, low tricycle to the front of the garage and was trying to open the big closed door. The boys hurried to give him a hand, but not even three of them could raise the door. It was locked.

"Try around at the side," Andy suggested. He picked up the Big Wheel, and Paco trotted behind him.

The side door was unlocked. They all went

in and Andy set the tricycle where Paco showed him, along the side of the car.

"I guess all ballplayers have nice cars," Andy said, tapping the rear fender with his forefinger. "Wonder why the 'For Sale' sign's on it. This is a good Cadillac, just about like Keith's."

"Hadn't you better look at the fender?" Andy asked in a nasty tone. "After all, you didn't miss Keith's. Better clear this one, too."

Jeff hesitated. He didn't like the unfriendly note that had come back into Andy's voice.

"*You* look," he said.

"All right, I will." Andy marched around the front end of the car as if he were going to fight a battle. "And when I tell you the fender is smooth, you'll have to say you're sorry."

Chapter 7

THE HIT-AND-RUN CAR

As Andy moved around the front of the car, Jeff glared at his back. He wasn't going to say he was sorry when the car turned out to be okay. He wanted to find the car that had hit Ted. Why should he be sorry just because Andy thought they shouldn't check a friend's car?

"What color was Ted's bike?" Andy interrupted Jeff's thoughts.

"Red. Why?" Jeff looked up curiously.

Andy was standing on the far side of the car, staring at the right front fender. Astonishment had drawn his mouth wide open.

"The fender is dented. Badly." Andy's voice sounded choked, the way it had when he came to say Ted was in the hospital. "And there's a kind of orange-red scratch on it."

Jeff hurried to the other side of the car and stared at the badly dented fender. He had wanted to find a long, pale car with a badly dented fender. Now he had, and he wished he had not. "I can't believe it," he said.

Long before the shock and dismay had had a chance to fade, Paco began tugging at his leg.

"Bed," Paco said. Then he added something Jeff couldn't understand. Maybe it was Spanish. "Bed," Paco said again.

"Okay, off to bed." Jeff bent to pick him up.

Putting a child to bed was a lot more complicated than Jeff had expected. To his relief there wasn't time to think about anything else.

They had to find the right pajamas and fold Paco's clothes the way he liked to leave them. They had to help him brush his teeth and give him exactly half a glass of water. They had to try to understand the mixture of Spanish and English that was his conversation.

The last thing to be done was the bedtime story. Each boy read one of Paco's favorite books. Luckily they were picture books and the words were English. They were easy and fun to read.

Almost an hour after they had started, Jeff and Andy left Paco lying peacefully in his bed with the side rails raised. They stood in the middle of the small living room.

It was a welcoming room with sand-colored walls and carpet. Bright, interesting Mexican objects such as painted wooden bowls and *papier mâché* animals filled the shelves and tables. Any other time they would have enjoyed examining things.

"Now what do we do?" Andy asked.

"Go back and look again to be sure we saw what we think we saw," Jeff suggested.

Silently, they opened the door to the garage, turned on the light, and walked around the long white Cadillac. The dented fender showed clearly, even in the dim glow of the overhead light.

"Do you really think it's possible Julio could have run over Ted?" Andy whispered, as if he were afraid someone would hear.

"He was hit right near here," answered Jeff. " I figure that if you cut through this backyard, you come to that vacant lot on Willow Lane. And that's next to the place where Ted got hurt."

"Let's go back inside," Andy said. "We don't want to be caught looking at this car."

Just as they entered the house again, the doorbell rang. Jeff looked at Andy and saw the same fear he felt.

What if it were the police? What if they had come to arrest Julio?

"We have to answer," Jeff whispered. "The bell will wake Paco if it keeps ringing."

Andy stared at him, his jaw clenched with horrible excitement. He nodded agreement, and they went to the door.

The man standing outside was tall and slim and very handsome. He wasn't wearing a police uniform. Instead, the white slacks and white knit shirt he wore seemed like clothes a television actor would wear.

Very dark brows arched over his black eyes as he inspected the boys, one brow raised in an impatient question. His eyes reminded Jeff of Penguin's eyes.

"Is Julio around?" the man asked. His voice was deep and hypnotic with only a trace of an accent like Julio's.

"He's gone out to dinner," Jeff told him.

"Dinner?" Both of the stranger's eyebrows rose and his thin mouth curved down. "I would not have thought he would have much appetite tonight."

"Well, he does," Jeff said quickly. He wasn't going to let some man he didn't know be critical of Julio. "Why shouldn't he?"

The man's mouth turned upward into a quick friendly smile. "You're right. Why shouldn't he? Look, I am Ernie Seville, a friend of Julio's. I left my raincoat here and I would like to get it."

"You're Ernie Seville?"

Jeff was amazed. This was the pitcher who had taken over for Julio in Saturday's game. Out of his baseball uniform, he looked a lot different.

The man seemed amused. "You have heard of me. Good. Then will you look in the closet for my white raincoat?" He smiled and winked. "Must I explain, too, that Keith Owen and I stopped here Friday night after we got back from Detroit? Teresa picked us up at the airport and cooked us a meal. When I left, I forgot the coat."

"You and Keith were here Friday night?" Jeff repeated foolishly. In his head he was adding two and two and getting a number he didn't like.

"I'll get the coat," Andy said. He rummaged in the closet to the right of the door and came up with the white raincoat.

"Thanks." Holding it over one arm, Ernie Seville reached for an inner pocket. He drew out two autographed pictures of himself and handed one to each of them. "Be sure to tell Julio I was here."

He swung down the steps and got into an old green Buick.

Jeff closed the door and locked it, his eyes wide. "Did you hear that? Keith was here that night. But he didn't say a word about it."

"Why should he have?" Andy asked.

"Teresa picked everyone up at the airport, so Julio must have given Keith and Ernie a ride home. It could have been about ten-thirty. What if they took Willow Lane on their way to the highway? And on the way, they could have run into a boy on a bicycle."

"Wow!" Andy seemed stunned. He sat down in one of the orange flower-patterned chairs in the living room. His foot swung madly.

Jeff paced back and forth across the middle of the small room, carried away by his imagination. "That's what could have happened. But I think if Keith had been there, he would have called the police. And what about Ernie? Ted was hit from behind, by a car heading south on Willow Lane. Julio would have been driving south as he came back home — after he had dropped off Keith and Ernie. If Julio was driving south on Willow, he would have been alone."

"I still don't understand why he wouldn't stop to help Ted," Andy said. "Julio doesn't seem like the kind of person who would do a terrible thing like that and run away."

"No, he doesn't," Jeff agreed. An astonishing thought crossed his mind. "But it sure explains one thing."

"What's that?" Andy wanted to know.

Jeff slumped onto the couch and dropped his picture of Ernie Seville onto the coffee table. "Now we know why Julio is pitching so badly. I would, too, if I had a hit-and-run on my conscience."

"It sure fits in," Andy breathed. A new expression of shock spread across his face.

"Running away is worse than having the accident in the first place," Jeff said. "I mean, an accident is bad, but it *is* an accident. Not telling, not helping, that's worse. Ted could have died if he hadn't been taken to the hospital."

Andy stared at him unhappily. "Are you going to call the police?"

Jeff noticed his friend said "you" not "we." Well, Jeff had to admit he was the one who had wanted to play detective. How could he have guessed it wouldn't be so very satisfying to find the car with the dented fender as he had thought it would be?

All the time he had been seeing himself triumphantly directing the police to the criminal, some unknown evil figure. Everyone he knew would have been impressed. His parents might have taken some time from their busy lives to be proud of him. Only now, telling on Julio seemed more like snitching on a buddy than doing a heroic deed.

"I don't know what to do," Jeff answered at last. "The police should know about Julio's car, but I don't want to tell them."

"I won't go with you." Andy's face set stubbornly. "I think there's some other explanation. You're just jumping to conclusions. I don't think Julio had anything to do with Ted being hurt."

"I have *not* jumped to any conclusion," Jeff protested. "Anyway, I know why you're saying that. You told me this afternoon we should mind our own business. That's why you don't want to go."

"Okay," Andy admitted. "Maybe it is."

"But everything points to Julio."

Andy remained unmoving. "But we don't have any *proof*. I remember one time my mom made some cookies for the Brownie meeting. One of us five kids ate the whole batch. We always thought my littlest sister ate them. She had been alone in the kitchen, and then later she wasn't hungry for lunch. It really looked as if she'd eaten those cookies, but since she never admitted it, there was no way to tell for sure."

"Okay," Jeff interrupted. He could feel himself turning as stubborn as Andy. "Only this isn't five kids and a cookie jar. This was a hit-and-run." He could hear his voice rising, and he stopped to get hold of himself.

"Look," he said after a minute, "you were talking about proof. We could tell Julio we know about the car. See what he has to say."

"Hey, yeah." Some of the stiffness left Andy's body. "I guess we could do that all right. And if he has a good explanation, we'll forget the whole thing, okay?"

Jeff was so certain that Julio couldn't explain that he agreed at once. "Okay. One of us gets him alone and —"

The sound of the door unlocking interrupted him. Keith and Julio and Teresa poured into the room, laughing and talking.

"Well you two certainly look gloomy," Keith said. "Anything go wrong?"

Before the laughter on Julio and Teresa's faces could fade, Andy said, "Oh, no. Everything's fine. Paco was really good."

Jeff didn't say a word. But he stood up, ready to ask Julio about the car right then. He tried to catch Julio's eye, but the young man was smiling happily at his wife. Keith had wanted to cheer them up and he had. How could Jeff possibly ask about the car at that moment?

"Look, guys," Keith said, "this has been great. But I have an interview with a reporter first thing in the morning. Got to go. Come on, boys."

So they left without talking to Julio. Jeff and Andy didn't even have a chance to consult again because Mrs. Ferguson came out to talk to Keith and sent Andy inside.

That night Jeff couldn't sleep. And he couldn't pay attention in school the next day.

Luckily, he had the afternoon off because of a teachers' meeting.

For once he was glad to get home to his quiet house. Until it was time to go to the game, he wanted to be alone to think. The more he thought, the more convinced he was that he was right.

Julio's car had a bad dent on its right front fender. Ted was hurt near his house. Julio was home because the game in Detroit was called, and he would have had to be out driving late in the evening to take Keith and Ernie home. After Julio had dropped the other players off, most likely he would be heading south on Willow Lane — alone. There might be no proof, but the evidence against him was awfully strong.

The telephone rang.

"Jeff?" asked a faint voice when he lifted the receiver.

"This is Jeff." His voice was gruff. "Who's this?"

"It's Ted."

"Hey, Ted!" Jeff whooped, relieved. "Is it really you? How do you feel?"

"Better. I wanted to thank you for the radio. I've been able to listen to the music for a couple of days now. And I see the ball games on TV. Sure makes the time go faster."

"Will you be out of the hospital soon?"

"Not for a while. My head still hurts a lot and the broken leg isn't good enough yet." Ted sounded weaker as he continued to talk.

"That's too bad. It seems funny around here without you."

"It was nice of you to come to see me. I'm sorry I couldn't talk very much." Ted didn't speak for a long moment. All Jeff could hear was the rasp of his breathing. Then he said, "You asked me about the accident, didn't you?"

"We wanted to help find the car that hit you," Jeff explained. A lump formed in his throat. How could he tell Ted they suspected who had hit him, and yet had said nothing to the police?

"The police haven't had much luck," Ted said. "No leads at all. At first I didn't remember much of anything to tell them. Now things are coming back. This morning

I remembered there might have been a witness to the accident."

"A witness?" Jeff caught his breath. "What do you mean?" He was terrified for Julio.

"Well, just before the car hit me, I passed a vacant lot." Ted's voice became stronger. "I saw a light and heard some noises. I thought it was kids camping."

Jeff's stomach tightened. Witnesses? What children could have been there? Why hadn't one of them come forward to tell what had happened? What if one of them *did* come forward?

"I have to go now," Ted said. "I'll call again in a few days."

Jeff hung up. He flopped into his mother's best cream-beige upholstered chair. He went over everything he knew, trying to put the parts together like a puzzle.

Only one new idea came to him. Keith was obviously calm and relaxed. So was Ernie. Julio was a nervous wreck. As far as he could see, that pretty well proved the hit-and-run had happened when Julio was alone on his way home.

Since they were going to the ball game that afternoon, he would tell Keith everything. Keith would know what to do.

He called to tell Andy his decision, and Andy agreed. In fact, his voice bubbled his relief.

"I wish we'd thought of that last night. Talk to him as soon as you can."

Chapter 8

CONFESSION

The ride to the ball park on Friday afternoon was exactly the same as it had been before, except the joy was gone.

Instead of trying to hide his gloom, Julio was openly sunk in it. He huddled in his seat like a child being punished. Jeff and Andy exchanged glances, neither of them feeling much better than Julio.

Only Keith was cheerful. He told jokes and asked trivia questions about baseball. He had to tell them most of the answers because nobody else even felt like making a guess.

By the time the car reached the ball park even Keith's good humor had faded away. He seemed grateful to be greeted by the smiling face of the parking lot man.

"Afternoon, Bob. Got any room for us?"

"I think I can fit you in." Bob smiled at the boys, seeming to remember them.

Keith parked and got out of the car, still talking to the attendant. Julio and Jeff and Andy got out on the other side.

"When shall we talk to Keith?" Andy whispered.

Jeff shook his head helplessly. "I don't know," he whispered back. "Do you think there'll be a chance before the game?"

"During batting practice, maybe. We could call him over." Andy's teeth were practically grating, he was holding his jaw so tightly.

They followed Keith and Julio up the ramp to the park entrance. The wooden door was standing open in the warm spring sunshine. Inside was a large open space. A wooden table with three chairs stood in the center.

Julio passed too close to one of the chairs,

hit a leg with his foot, and stumbled. The book he was carrying under one arm flew from his grasp and slid across the floor. Several sheets of paper spilled out.

With a mutter in Spanish the boys couldn't understand, Julio bent to pick them up. Keith and Andy kept walking. Jeff stopped. Here was the chance to talk to Julio he had wanted the night before. Why not take it?

"Julio, could I talk to you?" he said quickly, before he lost his nerve.

"Sure." Julio stood up, holding papers in one hand and book in the other. "This is my lesson for the school. I learn the English, you see."

Three players passed them with a nod, on their way to the dressing room. Normally, Jeff would have been thrilled to be that close to any members of the team. Now he was anxious for them to be out of the way.

"Julio—" Jeff started out with the sternest tone he could manage, "—did you know that Andy's and my best friend was hit by a car last Friday night?"

"Yesss, I hear this." Julio stiffened. His eyes were as wide and dark as rain puddles at night. They seemed to reflect the room.

It wasn't easy, but Jeff kept his eyes on Julio. Much as he wanted to, he couldn't let himself look at the floor or anywhere else. He had to look at Julio.

"The police are looking for the car that hit our friend. The driver didn't stick around after it happened. The police know, though, that he had a long, light-colored car."

Julio winced. "There is some reason you tell me this, yes?"

Jeff planted his feet wide apart. The words he had planned to say stuck in his throat. It wasn't too late. He could still change the subject. But could he ever face Ted again ?

He cleared his throat. "I think I found that car last night in your garage."

For a long moment he didn't think Julio was going to make any reply. The pitcher formed a neat pile of his homework papers and replaced them in his English book. Then he tucked the book back under his arm.

"You tell this to police?" Julio asked.

"Not yet," Jeff admitted.

He stopped, aware that he should be asking questions, not answering them. All he had done was warn Julio so he could get rid of the car.

"Did you know there was a witness to the hit-and-run?" he asked quickly. That would make Julio think twice.

It did. The mirrorlike blankness of Julio's eyes shattered. He looked scared to death. "You know this?" he exclaimed.

"You mean you knew already about the kids in the vacant lot?" Jeff felt bewildered, as if he had missed something.

"Some persons? In a lot?" Julio sagged into the chair that had tripped him. He cradled the English book in his lap, unaware that it was there. "I do not know about some persons in a lot." His head drooped.

"Well, whoever they are, they haven't said anything yet." Jeff couldn't help it, he wanted to reassure Julio.

He had expected Julio might get angry when he heard what Jeff knew. But, instead, Julio seemed crushed.

"If you really did it," Jeff said in a faint voice, "why did you have to run away?"

"Because I must. No thing else to be done." Julio didn't raise his head.

"I have to tell. I don't want to get you in trouble, but I have to tell." Jeff felt tears filling his eyes.

"Maybe you could confess, Julio. It won't be so bad if you go to the police and tell them what happened. It was an accident. They won't be too hard on you if you turn yourself in."

"Confess?" Julio whispered. He raised his head and Jeff saw his eyes were wet. "It is possible. I could confess." Licking his lips, he nodded his head. "Yes, I could confess. After the game I will do it."

"You will?" Incredible relief erupted through Jeff. Maybe he had done the right thing after all. Maybe it would be all right.

But he felt even more sorry for Julio. Suddenly he understood how desperate the ballplayer must feel. Maybe it would help if he offered to go to the police with him.

As he was about to say so, a deep voice broke in. "Hey! What's going on here? Giving autographs, Julio?"

Ernie Seville was approaching from the parking lot door. Julio sprang to his feet. Jeff brushed at his eyes with his knuckles.

"My friend comes to enjoy the game," Julio said. He swallowed and his thin throat jumped.

His eyes narrowed, Ernie Seville stared at Jeff. "Yes, I saw you last night, did I not?" With a friendly smile he explained to Julio about having come to pick up his raincoat.

Not much interested, Julio distractedly fingered his book. "It is late," he interrupted. "We must go to dress."

"Sure," Ernie agreed. "If the starter is as nervous as you, I will be working up a sweat in the bullpen before three innings have passed."

They all started toward the dressing room. When they reached it, Julio waved his hand sadly and disappeared inside. Ernie Seville paused a moment to wink at Jeff. Then he, too, went inside.

Jeff wandered along the hall past the ushers' lockers, looking for Andy. Most of the ushers were already wearing their blue and gold uniforms. They were getting their instructions for the game that night.

Andy was waiting on the ramp that over-looked the ball park. "What happened?" he demanded as soon as Jeff appeared. "Did you talk to him about the accident?"

"I told Julio we saw the car in his garage."

"You did?" Andy's cheeks blazed with excitement. "What did he say?"

"He said he'd confess to the police after the game."

"No kidding," Andy said. "Why does he want to wait until after the game?"

"I don't know," Jeff admitted. "Maybe he just has to get used to knowing he has to tell."

Andy nodded as if that sounded reason-able to him. "Well, I guess we can enjoy the game then. We've done everything we can."

They watched batting practice. When it was time, they went to their seats.

"Hello, boys. Nice to see you again."

Turning around, Jeff looked into Mr.

Propper's smiling face. Beside him was a small woman with white hair, Mrs. Propper. And behind the woman were Teresa and Paco and Allison, carrying the ever-present Penguin.

Oh no, was all Jeff could think. How could he sit there all evening with Teresa and Paco, of all people?

Now he had another idea why Julio had wanted to wait before he confessed. He wanted Teresa and Paco to see him in his uniform one last time. What would happen when they found out about him? Jeff winced.

He concentrated on saying a polite hello, and Andy did the same. Mr. Propper introduced Mrs. Propper. Paco came to sit on Jeff's lap. Allison and Penguin plopped on Andy, much to his disgust.

Soon Andy's parents joined them. Everyone laughed and talked a lot. Nobody seemed to notice that Jeff didn't have anything to say.

After a time Paco slid out of Jeff's arms. He climbed over Mrs. Propper's legs to get to his mother.

"It's only one of Julio's games that would

drag Mr. Propper away from his telescope," Mrs. Propper was saying to Teresa. She lifted Paco over her right foot. "Mr. Propper thinks the world of Julio. He'd do anything for him."

Jeff raised his head to listen. He didn't know Mr. Propper was that fond of Julio. "He'd do anything for him." Jeff had heard someone else say almost the same thing recently. Who had said it?

Straightening his shoulders uneasily, Mr. Propper said, "I think I'll go get hot dogs for the youngsters." He headed for the refreshment stand.

Jeff had a strong hunch, and he wanted to ask Mr. Propper about it.

"Maybe he could use help bringing things back," said Jeff. He jumped up and followed Mr. Propper.

Although Mr. Propper seemed surprised, he accepted Jeff's offer of help. They plunged through the crowd to the hot-dog stand. A lot of people had the same idea, and they had to wait at the end of a long line.

Jeff didn't mind. It was a beautiful warm night. Friday night had been just as nice the week before. The night was perfect for looking at the stars, too — just as it had been a week before.

His stomach felt as if someone was using it for a curve ball, but Jeff didn't hesitate. The conversation he expected with Mr. Propper couldn't be any harder than the conversation he'd had with Julio. And the awful thing he had said to Julio was no worse after the words had been spoken than it was before.

"I guess you were out looking at stars last week after it got dark," Jeff began.

Mr. Propper looked uncomfortable. He didn't answer.

"I guess you saw Julio run over that kid on a bicycle last Friday night." Jeff's hands were shaking so badly he had to put them in his pockets. "Why didn't you call the police, Mr. Propper?"

"I don't know what you're talking about," Mr. Propper said. His little mustache twitched.

"It was about ten-thirty," Jeff insisted. "You were there with your telescope in the vacant lot. My friend who was hit saw you."

It wasn't quite the truth, but almost. Ted had told him he thought kids were in the vacant lot. No children had come forward. Jeff thought now that was because no children had been in the lot. Instead, a man had been there — Mr. Propper.

He knew he was right — only what if he was wrong?

Chapter 9

WHAT THE WITNESS SAW

The silence lasted a long time.

"All right," Mr. Propper said at last. His mustache wiggled even more frantically. "I was there."

I've figured it out! Jeff thought, in excitement. But he knew he mustn't let the triumph show. Not yet.

"What did you see?" he asked, forcing himself to be calm.

"I was looking at the stars," Mr. Propper told him. "They were so fascinating I completely forgot I'd promised my wife I'd be home early. As soon as I noticed the time, I began to pack up my telescope. That was when I noticed the light of a bicycle passing."

His fingers toyed with the buttons on his sport shirt. Jeff stared at him hard, willing him to go on.

"Then I heard the car come around the corner," Mr. Propper continued. "It raced along Willow Lane, much too fast. I saw the bicycle swerve, then I saw the car hit it."

The hot-dog line moved forward, and Mr. Propper moved with it.

"The car zoomed away," Jeff prompted, staying close beside him. "But not before you realized that it was Julio's."

"The car didn't zoom away," Mr. Propper corrected him. "It stopped and backed up. I had turned away to run for help. When I looked back, a man was bent over the boy lying in the road. I couldn't be sure, because taillights aren't very bright — but I thought I recognized Julio." He smoothed at his mustache, arranging the short hairs fussily.

"Julio got out?" Jeff asked, surprised.

Mr. Propper nodded. "He picked up the boy and carried him over to the grass and set him down. After that he went back to the car. It drove off before he was all the way inside."

"And that was all?"

"That was all."

Something about the story bothered Jeff, but he couldn't put his finger on it. Before he could ask more questions, the line moved forward again and they reached the counter. Mr. Propper looked strained, but he managed to order the hot dogs. Jeff put relish and mustard and catsup on all but his own.

After Mr. Propper paid, they started back. The old man didn't say anything more about the hit-and-run.

"Is that all?" Jeff asked as they approached their section.

Mr. Propper sighed like Jeff's mother did when he bothered her after a hard day at work. He stopped walking. "No, that's not all. I called the police and told them about the boy lying on the grass. I guess they thought I was another motorist who had happened by. I didn't tell them I actually saw the accident."

"But why didn't you?" Jeff persisted. "I'm sorry, but I don't understand."

"I wasn't absolutely certain the man I saw was Julio. It would be a terrible thing to accuse the wrong person." Mr. Propper bit his lip. "If it *was* Julio, I didn't want to be the one who got him into trouble. And I guess I didn't want to spoil my peaceful retirement by testifying at any trial."

"What if Ted had died?" Jeff asked. "Would you have said something then?"

"He didn't die," Mr. Propper said. "And I'm never going to say anything. You'd better not, either. Your friend is going to be all right, so think of Julio. He's just getting started in the big league. His career would be ruined if he were arrested. That's what he must have thought of after it happened. And after all, it was partly the boy's fault. He fell into the path of the car. Kids shouldn't be riding bikes after dark, anyway."

One hot dog began to slip out of Jeff's hands. He jabbed it back with his chin. Mr. Propper headed for their seats again. He walked so fast Jeff could hardly keep up with him.

After they handed around the hot dogs, Jeff sat down and took a bite of his. How could he tell Andy what he had just found out?

Should he take Mr. Propper's advice and never say anything to anyone? Before he knew it, the hot dog was gone. He hadn't even tasted it.

Would Julio's career be ruined if people knew what he had done? Now he could picture the newspaper headlines. "Ballplayer Hit-and-Run Driver." "Sox Pitcher Goes to Jail." Pictures of Teresa and Paco would be on the front page along with articles about what had happened.

The awful image faded, and Jeff noticed that all the players were lined up on the field. He shivered and looked for Julio. There he was, standing beside Keith. They were talking. During the entire national anthem they hardly stopped their conversation. Even from so far away Julio looked white-faced and scared.

"Do you think Julio told Keith about what happened?" Andy asked in a whisper. "I'm worried about him. Maybe we should have told Keith everything. He's Julio's best friend on the team."

Jeff didn't say anything because another

possibility had occurred to him. Suddenly he remembered someone else, besides Mr. Propper, who had been ready to do anything for a friend. It had been Julio talking about Keith.

The game began, and Jeff forgot to watch. Instead, he was thinking hard, going over every word Mr. Propper had said. He tried to picture every detail. He came back to the same thing every time he went through the story: *the car was beginning to move away from Ted before Julio had jumped back in.*

Jeff nudged Andy's shoulder. "Can we get a message to Julio somehow?"

"A message to Julio?" Andy looked blank. "Can't it wait? This is the top of the fifth. The game won't go on that much longer."

"The fifth inning!" Jeff couldn't believe it. Had he really been that involved with his thoughts?

"I didn't think you were paying attention," said Andy. "The Indians are ahead four to one. Our starting pitcher was in trouble right away. And this relief pitcher has two men on and one out. Julio was sent down to the bullpen. I guess they figured he didn't last very long yesterday, so maybe they can use him again today."

Frowning, Jeff looked toward the corner where the pitchers warmed up. The slight figure of Julio was easy to spot.

"I *have* to talk to him before the end of the game," said Jeff. "Before he goes to the police. I just figured something out."

"What?" Andy's eyes widened.

"Come on," Jeff said. "Let's get away from here so we can talk."

"Okay," Andy agreed.

"It's really important. We *have* to think of a way to get to Julio."

After explaining to Andy's parents that they wanted to wander around, they received permission to go. Paco and Allison thought exploring sounded fun, but Teresa said the little ones had to stay. Before he and Andy left, Jeff whispered one short question to Mr. Propper. A shocked Mr. Propper nodded his head, agreeing with what Jeff said.

Jeff let out a long, satisfied breath and turned away with Andy.

As soon as they were out of hearing range of Andy's parents, Andy stopped. "Okay, what's going on?"

Jeff told Andy everything he had learned from Mr. Propper. He told the last part twice. "The car stopped after it hit Ted. Somebody got out and tried to help him."

"That sounds like something Julio would do," Andy agreed.

"The person who tried to help got back in the car on the right-hand side." Jeff cocked his head to watch Andy's reaction. "I just checked with Mr. Propper. Before the man Mr. Propper saw was in, the car started."

Andy frowned. "I don't get it."

"The right side isn't where the driver sits. It's where the passenger is. The man Mr. Propper thought was Julio was a *passenger*.

"You mean, Julio wasn't driving?" Andy still seemed puzzled.

"Right. That's why we can't let him confess," Jeff continued. "Julio's innocent. I think he's protecting somebody else."

The batter hit a long ball just then and they both watched as Cleveland runners crossed the plate. "Eight runs," Andy muttered. "We won't win now."

It began to worry Jeff that he had been right exactly two times. First, as soon as he saw that car in Julio's garage, he had known it was the one that had caused the accident.

The second time he had been right was when he had figured out that Mr. Propper had made the noise Ted had heard in the vacant lot. Jeff wasn't sure he could stand being right a third time, though. He didn't want to be right this time.

Andy asked the question he had been waiting for. "Who else could have been there?"

"It could have been either Keith or Ernie, but I think that Julio is protecting Keith."

The stubborn look started to spread across Andy's face.

Before he could argue, Jeff said, "I heard Julio say he would do anything for Keith."

"So you think Julio would take the blame for Keith?" Andy asked quietly.

Jeff nodded.

"So do I." Andy looked unhappily across

the playing field. "Hey, look! They're bringing in Julio to pitch."

Jeff swung his head to see. Andy was right. The new pitcher was Julio.

While Julio tossed his warm-up pitches they waited quietly, wondering what to do next.

Distracted as Jeff was, he had to notice the batter coming up. The first man Julio had to face was the Indians' most dangerous hitter.

How could Julio pitch, knowing he was going to the police to give himself up as soon as the game was over? How could he pitch, knowing he would take the blame for something he hadn't done?

But Julio wasn't pitching like a man whose career would soon be over. He struck out the feared batter. Jeff and Andy stared. The next man up popped the first pitch to the catcher. The Indians were retired.

"Well," Andy said, "he did okay. But I don't know how you're going to talk to him now."

"He'll be in the dugout while the Sox are batting." Jeff tried to plan ahead. "He doesn't bat because of the designated hitter rule. You know — in this league the pitcher doesn't go to the plate. Could we get a note to him while he's in the dugout?"

"Maybe." Andy considered that. "He'll be sitting on the bench or resting in back. I'll try to attract Keith's attention and have him give your note to Julio. He can go into the dugout."

"No," Jeff said quickly, "not Keith. We can't let Keith know yet what we're up to."

"Okay," Andy agreed. He searched through his pocket and pulled out a fat yellow pen. "Here's a marker. Do you have paper?"

"Never carry the stuff." Jeff gave him a weak grin and accepted the pen.

"Wait a minute." Andy made a dive behind a concrete post. "How about this?" He handed Jeff a smudged and partially used score card.

"Better than nothing." Jeff gripped the pen and scratched a message on the card, "Have to see you right away. Meet me outside dressing room. Jeff." He handed it to Andy.

"We don't dare wait until the game is over. Get this to Julio somehow. I'll go inside and wait by the dressing room door. Julio should be able to get away for a minute, and that's the only place we can talk."

Andy read the note and folded it in half. While the crowd rose for the seventh-inning stretch and sang encouragement to the team, the boys went their separate ways.

Getting into the off-limits area beneath the stands wasn't as difficult as Jeff had expected. He just ducked into the corridor during the round of applause when the first Sox batter came out.

As he marched toward the dressing room, he heard cheers coming from outside. He hoped the Sox were getting some runs to catch up and win the game for Julio.

Something good needed to happen to cheer Julio. Especially if Jeff's new theory turned out to be right. He was shocked by what he had figured out, but he was sure Mr. Propper's advice was wrong.

It wasn't a good idea to sit back and say nothing. There had been a crime. If he could name the guilty person, that was what he had to do.

When he reached the door to the dressing room, Jeff leaned against the wall and casually stuck a hand in his pocket. He hoped that he didn't look as nervous as he felt. It seemed as if Julio was taking forever to get there.

After checking the time, he began to pace up and down. He went as far as the table where he had talked to Julio and sat down.

"Well, here you are," someone said. It wasn't Julio. "You are Jeff, are you not? Julio sent me to talk with you."

The man who came out of the shadows was Ernie Seville.

Jeff stood up quickly, remembering that Ernie was Julio's friend.

Ernie Seville smiled. He looked more like a television actor than a ballplayer. "Your friend threw a note to me and called that it was for Julio. I gave it to Julio, but he would not come. He sent me to talk to you."

Jeff hesitated. He was sure Julio would have come if he could have. If he had sent Ernie, it was because he trusted him.

Chapter 10

JEFF IN DANGER

"I know Julio wasn't driving the car the other night." Jeff said.

"Is that so?" Ernie asked, smiling again. "And what car is that?"

Ernie didn't know anything about the hit-and-run, Jeff decided. So he had to be very careful and give Ernie the message for Julio in a way that wouldn't give away too much.

"Tell Julio I can prove he was only a passenger," Jeff said. His hand ruffled through his hair as he paused. That might have told too much.

"A passenger?" Ernie Seville came nearer until he was standing directly across the table from Jeff. "Only a passenger where?"

"Tell him it will be all right," Jeff continued. "We have to do that errand together after the game because I can help him."

He couldn't think what more could be said. Suddenly he noticed Keith Owen waiting silently where Ernie had stood a moment before. What was Keith doing here? The game couldn't be over so soon.

Catching Jeff's eye, Keith shook his head slowly. Jeff frowned, not understanding. Keith put a finger to his lips.

So that was it. Keith didn't want Ernie to know he was there. Jeff wasn't going to let him get away with that one. Keith was taking advantage of Julio by letting Julio take the blame for the accident. He was using their friendship to keep himself out of trouble. No wonder he had taken Julio to dinner when the pitcher had shown signs of cracking. No dinner was enough to help Julio. Only the truth could do that.

"Hello, Keith," Jeff said loudly.

Keith scowled in disgust.

Ernie whirled and stood still, balancing most of his weight on one leg. "You have walked out on the game, Keith?" he asked. "That is likely to earn you a fine. And after you have just hit a grand-slam home run, too." He moved casually around the corner of the table.

A grand slammer? Four runs for the Sox and I missed it! Jeff thought.

"Couldn't be helped." Keith cut the words short. "I had to talk with Jeff here."

I'll bet, Jeff thought, glad Ernie was there.

With a soft laugh Ernie glided around another corner of the table so he was behind it with Jeff. "Is that not odd? I had the very same idea."

Something was happening that Jeff didn't understand.

The next moment he understood even less. Ernie Seville grabbed him and held him tightly in front of his chest. The pitcher's slender arms were as strong as steel cables. Why should Ernie be grabbing him? It was *Keith* who had committed a crime, wasn't it?

And suddenly Jeff understood all too well.

He had made a terrible mistake. After thinking it all out, getting every move in its place, he had known that Julio had not been driving the car that had hit Ted.

So Jeff had assumed Julio was protecting the driver—Julio's best friend, Keith.

How wrong he had been!

Ernie Seville had been the driver of the car.

"You did it!" Jeff cried out loud.

The arm around him tightened painfully. Fear gripped him with the same force.

"I had poor, innocent Julio right where I wanted him." Ernie's voice rumbled in Jeff's ear, his mouth was so close. "And then these crazy kids have to come along and spoil it all."

"Let the boy go," Keith ordered.

Ernie took a step toward the open door to the parking lot, dragging Jeff with him. "The kid is my ticket out of here."

"You don't have to be quite that desperate." Keith didn't sound especially concerned. To Jeff he said, "Julio told me everything just before the game started. Then a few minutes ago, Andy almost dived into the dugout to let me know Ernie didn't give Julio your message. I figured you might be in trouble, so I hustled over here. We'll have to rescue Andy later from the usher who grabbed him, but I thought that could wait."

As he talked, Keith took two slow steps toward them. "Let's talk to a security guard, Ernie. Don't worry, you'll be treated fairly."

"I would not be worried if I were like you," Ernie growled. "You have been two years in Baltimore, and now here you are a star. Big home run hitter."

He laughed harshly. "This is my fourth year and I am not a star. I make it to starting pitcher and then they get a hot-shot rookie—that Julio—who takes my place."

"Is that why you tried to blame Julio?" Keith asked. "So you could get rid of him?"

"It should have happened that way." Ernie

shifted his position, but Jeff was still tightly pinned by the pitcher's muscular arm.

"Julio is afraid after the accident happens," Ernie continued. "I said it was his car, and I would swear he was the driver. They would believe me. The foolish little Julio can hardly speak English."

"They would *not* believe you." Jeff regained some of his courage. "I can prove Julio wasn't driving the car."

His breath left him with a gasp as Ernie Seville squeezed his chest viciously.

"Shut up! If you had not meddled, everything would have been well. Julio was so nervous he could not pitch. He was on his way straight back to the minors, and they would have had to make me a starter again."

"They would have brought someone else up," Keith told him. He took another casual step forward.

"The manager likes you in the bullpen. He thinks you're a great short-term pitcher and he's told you so. I've heard him. But you were so jealous of Julio, you wouldn't listen."

"It makes no difference. I am taking this

boy and will get away from here. At least I can get back to my home. I will not rot in some lousy jail."

Ernie Seville gave Jeff another jerk that hauled him off his feet as Ernie strode toward the open door. Just as they took the first step outside, Jeff began to struggle. He wasn't going to some strange place with a creep like Ernie Seville.

The abrupt angle of the ramp they were going down, and Jeff's jerking movements, threw Ernie off balance. As Ernie caught himself, Jeff twisted furiously and pulled at Ernie's fingers. The tight grip loosened. With a lunge, Jeff was free. He tumbled down the ramp.

At the bottom he came to a stop, out of breath and hurting. As Ernie started after him, Keith threw himself at Ernie. They both went down. Ernie struggled to escape but Keith gave him a hard punch in the mouth.

Ernie crumpled and fell. As he did, Bob, the man who took care of the cars, came running from the parking lot.

"Get the guards fast!" Keith ordered.

Rising to his knees, Ernie looked around. Keith stood over him, threatening to hit him again. Ernie's shoulders slumped, and he put his hands over his face. Ushers and security men started arriving in answer to Bob's call. Keith explained quickly what had happened.

As soon as the guards took charge of Ernie, Keith ran down the ramp to Jeff. "Hey, are you okay?" Real worry shadowed his face.

A funny feeling rippled through Jeff as he saw the ballplayer's concern. He wanted to cry. He hadn't thought Keith would be that worried about him. Not after he had suspected Keith of driving the hit-and-run car.

He tried to think of something happy. A loud roar from inside the stadium helped him. He managed a weak smile and stood up. "Sounds like we're getting a few more runs."

Keith grinned back. "We'll pull it out now that Julio's pitching like himself again." He gave Jeff a hand. "Let's go rescue Andy from the ushers. And then I'm going to have to try and explain to the manager why I'm not in the outfield right now."

They found Andy in the ushers' area, listening to the game on a radio. Jeff was amazed to find it was only the ninth inning. He felt as if hours had passed since he last saw Andy.

"Ernie was the one who did it," Jeff shouted.

"Ernie!" Andy jumped up excitedly. "I thought so! You know, Jeff, I did some thinking myself. My mom said that Keith lives within walking distance of Julio. Maybe Keith *walked* home the night of the accident. Maybe Julio wasn't protecting Keith after all.

"Then, when I asked Ernie to give the note to Julio, I got worried. Ernie pretended to give Julio the note, but I could tell he really dropped it into the dust. After he headed for the dressing room, I began to think you could use a little help. I just knew Keith wasn't guilty, and I decided I'd better trust my feelings and tell Keith where you were."

Andy grinned. "I risked life and limb to get to Keith. The manager's really mad because I tried to get into the dugout. When do you think we can talk to Julio?"

The next hour was the most confusing time the boys had ever known. Police talked to them, and so did reporters. All Jeff and Andy wanted was to talk to Julio, but they never got near him. As soon as the game was over, Julio and Keith and Ernie were taken away in police cars.

"We don't know what's going on," Andy complained when his parents were allowed to drive them home. "Nobody will tell us anything. What will happen to Julio now?"

Jeff was concerned about Julio's family. So were Jeff's parents when he explained to them what had happened. But they were more concerned that he hadn't told them what was going on. They had a long talk, and it was very late before Jeff got to bed.

"Good morning!" Someone was calling. Jeff tried to ignore the rap on his door. He would have gone back to sleep if he hadn't opened one eye enough to see Julio peering at him. In one second Jeff was wide awake.

"Julio!" he said happily. "How'd you get here? What did the police say?"

"So many questions." Julio was grinning his shy grin. "Keith and I have the thought we should talk together some little bit. He and Andy are out in Keith's car."

Jeff was out of bed and dressed in two minutes. They went outside to meet Keith and Andy.

"Tell me the whole thing from the very beginning," Jeff ordered.

The young pitcher laughed. "It begins with the rained-out game in Detroit. Keith and Ernie come to my house for a Mexican supper. And after we eat, Keith leaves. He walks home because he lives so near."

"Keith left?" Jeff looked relieved. "Then he really didn't know anything about the hit-and-run."

"I wish I had known," Keith said. "I would have put a stop to Ernie's scheme before it even got started."

"Where are we going?" Jeff wanted to know. "We don't have to talk to the police again, do we?"

The men laughed and got into the car. Julio held a white paper bag in his lap. Afraid he might be left behind, Jeff jumped in, too.

"We're going to see Ted," Andy said as they whizzed around the first corner. "Isn't that a great idea? Keith thought of it. He even got permission for all of us to see Ted."

When they got to the hospital, a different woman in a bright pink coat gladly gave them passes. She asked the ballplayers for autographs.

In Room 311 Ted was sitting up in bed, wearing his glasses. His long, solemn face broke into a smile when he saw them.

At first everyone talked at once and nobody heard a word. Then Jeff and Andy calmed down enough to introduce Ted and Keith and Julio.

"How'd you guys catch on to Ernie Seville?" Ted asked. "I heard about it on the radio."

"It was Jeff who figured it out," Andy said. "I just helped."

"Helped!" Jeff said. "You sure did. If you hadn't sent Keith after me, I don't know what would have happened."

"It is good he will not hurt anyone again

soon," Julio told them. " Ernie is dangerous ."

"He was dangerous because he wanted too badly to succeed." Keith settled on the foot of Ted's bed. "He couldn't stand to see Julio take what he had decided was his place on the team. When the accident happened, he tried to turn it to his own advantage. He didn't have a thought for the boy who might have been killed by his carelessness. You, Ted."

They took turns telling Ted what had happened. As the story progressed, Ted's sleepy eyes widened to semi-awake.

"Ernie says he must drive my car — with me along as a passenger — because maybe he will buy it," Julio explained. "The car is for sale because Teresa must have a smaller one. Ernie is driving around the neighborhood when he hits your friend Ted."

He seemed unable to say more, so Keith continued. "Ernie would have driven off without stopping. Julio made him go back. So Ernie waited with the motor running while Julio carried Ted to the side of the road. When he said they had to call for help, Ernie threatened him."

"It is my shame to have let him do this," Julio confessed, looking at the floor. "He tells me no one will believe I did not drive. Who am I? I have only one friend, Keith. Ernie has been in the country longer, so he will be believed. He says, I can find no help. I will be arrested. I will never pitch again."

"But you have lots of friends," Andy said. "All of us here. And Mr. Propper." He told Ted how Mr. Propper had seen the accident, but had tried to protect Julio.

"Tell Ted how you could prove Julio wasn't the driver of the car because of what Mr. Propper told you," Andy said.

"Well, it was kind of like a riddle," Jeff began. "Mr. Propper thought he recognized Julio in the lights from the back of the car. That got him so upset, he didn't pay much attention to what he saw after that. He never noticed someone else was driving."

"Julio came and talked to me, and a motor was running," Ted said. "I think I remember hearing that."

"You did." Jeff said. "I finally thought to ask Mr. Propper on which side of the car Julio had opened the door. Mr. Propper had never thought about it before, but he was certain it was the passenger's side."

"If Julio had been driving, he'd have got out on the left," Andy added. "Why slide across the seat when he was in a hurry?"

"That's what I thought." Jeff should have smiled, but instead he frowned. "I was so proud of myself for noticing that I got careless. I knew Julio would do almost anything for Keith, and I decided he'd lie about the hit-and-run to protect him. I was dumb not to check that out more. If Keith hadn't saved me, I could have been kidnapped by Ernie Seville."

"You could never have known what a bad man Ernie is," Julio consoled him. "All he saw was a chance to advance himself and to make trouble for me."

"You did a fine job, Jeff," Keith said. "In your own way, you solved the case. Now that this has been settled, I have a feeling Julio is going to be a winning pitcher again, starting with that save last night."

He reached inside his pocket and took out

three cardboard squares. "That's one reason the manager wants all you boys to have these season passes." He handed them around.

"Hey, terrific!" Jeff and Andy said together. Ted smiled a long solemn smile.

"Our manager is one good man, you know? said Julio. "He helps us with the police. And he makes only a small fine for Keith missing two innings of the ballgame."

Julio brought over the white paper bag he had left by the door. "And we bring donuts and milk to eat here for celebration." He spread out the donuts and poured milk.

Ted grabbed a fat chocolate donut as if it were the first real food he had seen in weeks. Andy took a frosted one, sniffing happily before he took a bite.

"Thanks, Julio." Jeff debated and then tried a cinnamon-coated one. It looked as if Keith and Julio had bought one of every flavor in the shop.

"Do not eat too much," Julio warned Jeff. "Your parents will come soon for you."

"My mom and dad and I are going to Lincoln Park Zoo to spend the day. And afterwards we're all going out to dinner." Jeff grinned with pleasure, thinking about his parents meeting him. No waiting alone in an empty house this time.

"We had a long talk when they heard about me and Ernie Seville. They think they should keep better track of what I'm doing. They said detective work could have got me in a lot of trouble."

The others laughed and nodded their heads.

Jeff laughed, too. "When is a detective not a detective?" he asked, eyes twinkling.

"When he's a policeman," guessed Andy.

"No," Jeff said, not waiting for the others to guess. "When he gives up detecting. And *I'm* the detective who's retiring."

"That's what I like about you," Ted said. His long face was solemn. "You know how to quit when you're ahead." And his face broke into the biggest grin Jeff had ever seen. "Thanks, friend."

About the Author

Carole Smith has been a baseball fan as long as she can remember. And since she seldom thinks of a story that's not a mystery, it's not surprising that she would combine the two interests to create a mystery about the world of professional baseball.

Carole lives in Grand Rapids, Michigan, with her husband, an engineer, and her two children. Carole's son shares her enthusiasm for baseball. Carole's daughter shares her interest in stories for children, often serving as her mother's best critic.

Working together with Ruth Hooker, Carole Smith has written two other mysteries for children: THE PELICAN MYSTERY and THE KIDNAPPING OF ANNA.

118734

DATE DUE

J
S
 Smith, Carole.
  The hit-and-run connection.